My Two Dogs
Their Two Stories

Stories by Christina J Donato

Illustrations by Alexander T. Lee

Table of Contents

Book One

The Saddest Dog Finds a Friend

Dedication

This book is dedicated to all the wonderful dogs

I have loved and will love.

Terri Featherhead 1966 – 1982

Belle 1982 – 1995

Hector 1985 – 1997

Bibi 1995 – 2010

Freckles 1997 – 2011

Grady 2009 – 2021

?

Chapter One: Meet Belle

The most friendly, adorable, playful dog lives in a little town on Long Island. Her name is Belle.

Belle is part beagle and part fox terrier. She has floppy ears and big, round, brown eyes. Her face is black, except for a white spot on one side of her nose that makes her look as if she was caught with her snout in a glass of milk and only had time to lick one side clean. On one side of her body, she is almost all white. On the other side, she has two black markings: one looks like a shoeprint, and one looks like a heart. Although Belle is three years old, she still looks and acts like a puppy … and hops like a bunny, jumps like a kangaroo, gallops like a horse, cries like a baby, purrs like a kitten, leaps like a frog, wiggles like a worm, and as clear as day can say, "Mommy." Yes, she can.

For as long as Belle can remember she has lived with her people. Even though they all love her very much, Belle is not always happy. You see, although she lives with four people, Belle is almost always alone.

Every morning at six o'clock, Mommy (whom Belle loves the most of all) wakes up and gives Belle her breakfast of a half of a cup of kibble and a dog biscuit. Then Mommy gives Belle a hug and a kiss and lets her out in the backyard for her morning romp. Belle romps alone, because Mommy is off to the office, then after that to night school, returning home so late in the evening that all she ever has time to do is give Belle a goodnight kiss and a quick belly rub before she goes to bed. On weekends Mommy sleeps late. When she is awake, she spends the day doing exercises and homework.

After Mommy leaves for work, Grandma wakes up and lets Belle in from outside. Grandma never has time to play because after she has her breakfast she does some reading, watches game shows and soap operas on TV, and then cooks dinner for her husband, Grandpa.

Grandpa works nights and sleeps during the day, waking up at three o'clock in the afternoon for his dinner.

Belle is happy when Grandpa gets up because she knows this means it is time for her dinner. Sometimes, if he is not too busy taking Grandma shopping or helping her with something, Grandpa may have a few minutes to play. Unfortunately, Grandpa plays too roughly and gets tired too quickly, so playtime doesn't last long. Before Belle knows it, it is six o'clock, and Grandpa must go to work.

There is one more person in Belle's family. She is Grandma's mother and Mommy's grandmother. Everyone calls her Nanny. Nanny lives in an apartment attached to Belle's house. Although Nanny is nice, the only thing she does all day is clean. Other than when Nanny gives Belle her nine o'clock bone in the morning and her four o'clock bone in the afternoon, Belle rarely sees her at all.

You can see that although Belle is the most friendly, adorable, and playful dog, she is also one of the saddest dogs.

Chapter Two: Belle the Happy Puppy

Belle wasn't always so sad. That is what makes it so terrible. Belle remembers how it used to be. When Belle first came to live with her people, she was only six weeks old and weighed 8 pounds. What a fuss they made over her! She was never alone all day long.

The first few nights, until Belle was used to her new home, Mommy had sat up with Belle until she fell asleep.

Everyone loved to be with puppy Belle. They petted her, kissed her, and hugged her. She got plenty of toys and her family loved to play. Most of all, they were always there when Belle needed them.

Oh boy, did she need them! As a puppy, Belle was always crawling under or behind things from which she couldn't get out. She was always eating things that would give her a bellyache. And bellyache after bellyache she had. Belle would eat bugs, sour apples that fell from the apple tree, leaves, wood chips, and most of all, paper. Belle would go after paper in any form: tissue, paper towels, napkins, food wrappers, cardboard boxes, and even money. Can you believe that she took a twenty-dollar bill right out of Grandma's purse? After that, Grandma never left her purse unzipped again.

However, of all the messes Belle got herself into, nothing compares with the time little Belle was just three months and playing with Mommy's four-year-old cousin. They were having a grand time running around the backyard when the boy suddenly fell on top of Belle. Belle let out a yelp so loud that everyone came running out of the house. The pain in her leg was too much for Belle to take. She was terrified. Gently, Mommy picked Belle up and took her straight to the animal hospital. Belle's leg was broken. The veterinarian was kind, which made Belle feel a little less frightened. To be sure her leg healed properly, and to be sure she did not move around too much, Belle had to stay at the animal hospital for a few days.

Finally, the day came to go home. When Belle got home, Mommy was there waiting. Mommy was so happy to have Belle back home that she snuggled her and cried, cried, cried, getting Belle's fur wet with her tears. Belle licked her mommy nonstop for just as long, to let Mommy know she was fine. And fine she was. The veterinarian had given Belle what he called "walking cast," But Belle was never on for merely walking. She hobbled and galloped and hopped around so much that her cast kept falling off and had to be replaced two times!

Getting her leg broken wasn't the only time Belle was in pain or frightened when she was a puppy. Well, you know how playful and bouncy Belle is. She's always ready to play with anything that moves, even if she must catch it, even if it's a bee. One time Belle was trying to catch a bee and it stung her upper lip. Ouch! The bee fell away but the stinger stayed behind. Belle tried to push it out with her paw, but that hurt. Sad and scared, Belle scratched the back door to the house and waited for someone to let her in. Grandpa did let her in, but he did not notice anything wrong. Belle just sat there by the door until Mommy walked by and saw her.

"Why are you just sitting there Belle?" asked Mommy. Belle lowered her head as Mommy stared at her.

Why doesn't she help me, Belle thought. *Can't she see what's wrong?*

Mommy bent over to lift Belle's face. There, as plain as day, did Mommy see one side of Belle's upper lip swollen to at least three times its normal size. She also saw the stinger. Although Mommy felt bad for Belle, the sight of Belle's swollen lip was so funny that she burst out laughing. Soon, the whole family was standing around Belle and laughing. Then, ever so gently, Mommy removed the stinger and cleaned the area. As she did so, Mommy talked softly, which helped Belle to be brave. Belle was so brave that she only whimpered once. For the rest of the day, everyone paid extra attention to Belle and she knew she was loved.

Things were so wonderful for Belle when she was a puppy that she didn't have to get hurt, or frightened, or even be bad to get attention. On her first Christmas, seven-month-old Belle was the center of attention. There was a Christmas stocking filled with presents for her under the Christmas tree. The stocking had Belle's name on it. Mommy had shown Belle the stocking and told her it was not to be emptied until Christmas morning. Every day until Christmas Belle checked the stocking to make sure it was still there. She was a good dog and waited until Christmas to open it. When the day finally arrived, Belle was the first one to get her stocking. She was even allowed to empty it herself, with a little help from Mommy. The stocking was filled with different toys and treats.

As Mommy, Grandma, Grandpa, and Nanny stood around making a fuss over Belle's presents, Belle ran off carrying the empty stocking with her.

A few months later, when Belle was eleven months old, Grandma and Grandpa went to a party. Even though they were away from Belle, she was still on their minds. They brought home two helium-filled balloons for her. What a treat! The balloons had long strings attached to them. As Grandpa let them go inside the house they soared toward the ceiling. Belle joyfully jumped, hopped, and skipped, trying to catch the balloons as Mommy took photographs and played with her. This was one of Belle's favorite puppy memories.

Chapter Three: Belle Grows Up

Just as children become adults, Belle the puppy grew up and became Belle the dog. Grown-up and 21 pounds, Belle's people no longer found her antics and mishaps so cute. Nanny began coming up with nicknames for Belle that weren't nice. She called her Troub-Belle, Mission Impossi-Belle, and Ding-a-ling-Belle. No longer did Belle's people run to her whenever she cried or whimpered, or not even when she said, "Mommy." When Belle was almost fourteen months, she was forced to learn to bark.

I bet you thought all dogs were born being able to bark. Well, not Belle. When she had not barked in her first few months Mommy was worried and told the veterinarian. He told her that some dogs may not bark until they are a year or so old.

On the day Belle first barked, she was outside and wanted to be let in. Her usual whimpering and hitting the door was getting her nowhere. Then, as Mommy and Grandma were making lunch, they heard a deep, hearty bark coming from the backyard.

"Who's that?" wondered Mommy, aloud. She went to the back door and saw Belle. She let Belle in.

Mommy was surprised. "Belle, how can such a small dog have such a big bark?"

Mommy was proud of Belle, so she told everyone about Belle's bark. Soon, Belle had many barks, from the high-pitched yap of a Chihuahua to the husky bark of a German Shepherd. Belle, as Mommy would say, was quite the impressionist.

The attention Belle got from learning to bark did not last long. It was probably the last fuss her family made over her. Belle had not noticed until the one morning Mommy let her outside for her morning romp. Belle thought it would be nice if she and Mommy would play hide and seek, so she hid beneath one of the bushes. She waited, but Mommy did not come looking for her. Nobody came looking for her. From that day on, Belle was pretty much alone.

Chapter Four: Dognapped!

After having her four o'clock bone, Belle is playing around outside. First, she kicks her ball, then she chases after it. She notices the gate to the front yard is open. Belle knows she shouldn't go in the front yard by herself. She has never been there alone before. However, she is tired of playing alone with the ball, so she goes through the gate anyway.

It is a bright, warm day. All the neighborhood children are out front playing. Belle cannot believe it! She loves children. Oh, how she wishes there was a child in her house. Children are never too busy or too tired to play.

Belle runs to the curb at the end of her lawn so she can get a closer look at the lively, joyful children.

"Hey, look at the dog!" shouts a little boy with red hair and freckles.

All the children begin to shout at once, "Come here, little dog! Little dog!"

Belle can't hold back. She hops across the

street and into the arms of the children. They pet, hug, and kiss Belle, giggling endlessly as they do.

"That tickles!" shouts a little girl as Belle licks her face.

"Lick me!" shouts another.

"No, me!"

All the children want her attention, and Belle is just the one to make sure they all get it. As they play, the children and Belle run farther and farther down the street. Before long, the children are being called home for supper. One by one they go until only the boy with the curly hair is left.

"You certainly are a playful pup," says the boy as Belle licks his hand. "I wish I could take you home with me." The boy thinks for a moment. He gets an idea. "Hey, wait a minute. I'll tell my mom and dad you followed me home and you don't belong to anyone. They'll have to let me keep you."

Belle doesn't understand what it is the boy

is saying to her. However, she likes the sound of his voice, so she feels safe.

"Then again, if they won't let me have a new bicycle, they'll be mean enough not to let me have you either," the boy continues. "We can try, though. But you are wearing ID tags, aren't you?" He reaches down to read the ID tags on Belle's collar. "So, your name is Belle."

Belle's ears perk up when she hears her name.

"When my parents see these tags, they'll know you belong to somebody. Unless ..." The boy looks around to make sure no one is watching. Then, he takes Belle's ID tags from her collar and slips them into his pocket. "Come on, Belle. I'll put your tags in my secret box under my bed so Mom and Dad will never be able to guess what I did." The boy runs off towards home. Belle happily follows.

When they reach the boy's home, he tells Belle to sit on the stoop while he goes inside the house. Belle has never been so tired in her whole life. She is glad to have the chance to rest. She curls up on the doormat and falls fast asleep. The next thing she knows, she is being carried into the house and put on a soft, fluffy towel near the curly-haired boy's bed.

Chapter Five: The Curly-Haired Boy

Suddenly, at 6 a. m., Belle sits up. At first, she doesn't remember where she is and begins to whimper. She finds her way to the front door, then barks and cries. The boy comes running.

"Mom," he calls, "I think the dog has to go out."

"Well then, let her out in the backyard," his mother calls back from the kitchen.

The boy tries to get Belle to follow him, but she doesn't move. She knows her mom is leaving for work now and she must get home to see that she leaves safely. The boy with the curly hair doesn't know this, so he picks her up and brings Belle to his backyard.

Belle quickly forgets Mommy Christina as she and the boy begin to play. The boy's dad comes out to play, too. As the boy and his dad toss a ball to each other, Belle jumps up to try and catch the ball in mid-air. She almost does a couple of times.

The boy and his parents eat dinner. Belle also has something to eat and a fresh bowl of cool water.

Later, the boy gets ready for bed. Before going to sleep, the boy reads to Belle from his favorite book, Clifford: The Big Red Dog. As he does, he stops to show Belle the pictures.

Hearing the boy read and seeing the pictures makes Belle remember her mommy. Sometimes during breakfast, Mommy reads Belle the comic strips with dogs in them. Sometimes she reads from a book of a collection of Peanuts comic strips, especially the ones with Snoopy in them. You see, Belle got her name because she is part beagle and one of Snoopy's sisters is named Belle. Mommy likes to pretend she was reading to Belle about her real brother.

After reading the story, the boy goes to sleep. Belle is restless for a while, thinking about Mommy, but she soon falls asleep right there next to the curly-haired boy's bed.

At exactly six o'clock the next morning, Belle wakes up. She runs to the bedroom door, but it is closed. She frantically scratches and paws at the door. She whines and barks to get out. The noise she makes wakes up the boy and both of his parents. Since it is Saturday, they are all angry at being awoken so early.

"Quiet, Belle," pleads the boy, as his mother opens the door to the bedroom. Belle darts out and runs straight for the front door.

"I hope she's not going to do this every morning," says the boy's mother.

"She won't be any trouble, Mom, I promise," says the boy as he runs to let Belle out in the backyard.

That day after lunch the boy decides to take Belle to the park, so they can have a lot of room to run around and play. As they're walking, the boy sees a reward sign on a telephone pole. It worries him.

The poster looks like this:

"Five hundred dollars," says the boy. "I could buy a new bicycle with that much money."

The boy with the curly hair looks down at Belle. She puts her front paws on the boy's leg and licks his hand.

"But to get the reward I'd have to give you back," he says to Belle.

The boy picks Belle up as tears fall down his face. Belle realizes something is wrong. She tries to comfort the boy by nuzzling his cheek. Then, Belle looks up at the reward sign and barks. The boy wipes his face.

"You're right, Belle," says the boy. "If anyone else sees this reward sign, I won't have you or the reward."

The boy pulls the reward sign down, folds it, and sticks it in his pocket. Just to be on the safe side, he decides to look around the neighborhood in case there are any more reward signs. He finds them everywhere. He saves one to keep in his secret box under his bed where he put Belle's ID tags. The rest he tears up and throws out.

Since it is now too late to go to the park, Belle and the boy head home for supper.

This evening, as the boy is getting ready for bed, his mom and dad say they hope Belle will not be waking them so early again tomorrow.

Unfortunately, Belle does wake them up every morning at 6 a.m. sharp. Also, each day at 9 a.m., 3 p.m., 4 p.m., 6 p.m., and 11 p.m. she cries and frets and scratches at the door for no reason at all. At least that is what the boy and his parents think. As the weeks pass, not even Belle is quite sure why she acts as she does. She loves the little boy and his mom and dad. They treat her well and give her a lot of attention. Yet each day at the same times she gets the feeling she has someplace else to be and something else to do. At the same times every day, Belle feels alone and sad.

Belle has now been with the curly-haired boy and his parents for three months. This morning it is the boy who wakes up first. That is because today is his birthday. He just cannot wait any longer to see his shiny, new bicycle. With Belle hopping along by his side, the boy runs to the den. That is where his parents always have his presents on his birthday mornings. However, a new bicycle is not there. The boy is surprised and disappointed.

"Of course, the bicycle isn't in the house," the boy says to Belle. "That would be silly."

Belle and the boy run to the front door and go outside. The new bicycle is not there. Belle runs to the garage door and hits it with her front paws. She barks.

"The garage!" shouts the boy. "It's just got to be in the garage!"

The boy opens the garage door. There is no new bicycle. Sad now, he tries to hold back the tears as he thinks of where else the new bicycle might be.

"Maybe it's in the backyard," says the boy to Belle.

They run around the house to the back. The boy does not want to get his hopes up or be disappointed. However, there is no new bicycle in the backyard either and he is disappointed anyway. He takes Belle into the house. His parents are in the kitchen waiting for them.

"There you are, birthday boy," says his mother as she bends over to kiss him. "Happy birthday, Honey."

"Happy birthday, big man," says his father, patting the boy on his back.

"Thanks, Mom. Thanks, Dad," says the boy, but he is not in the birthday mood.

"This is for you," says his mother, handing him a gift-wrapped box with his gift inside.

The boy opens the box and finds a pair of pants and a sweatshirt in his favorite colors: blue and orange. He thanks his parents and kisses them. Then, he closes the box and goes to put it in his room. His father stops him.

"Wait a minute," says the father. "Why are you so down today?"

"Because," says the boy, holding back tears, "today is my birthday and I didn't get a new bicycle. That's why."

"I told you I wouldn't get you a bicycle because the one you have is good enough."

"But it's my birthday."

"I'm sorry. We can't afford it, especially now since we have the dog."

The boy looks down at Belle and shouts at her, "It's all your fault, you stupid dog!"

The boy runs to his room and Belle follows. The boy slams the door shut before Belle can get into the room. Why did he yell at her? Belle does not understand. She paws at the door and whines.

Inside the bedroom, the boy reaches under his bed to get the box in which he hid Belle's ID tags and reward sign.

"If I brought Belle back, I could use the $500 to buy a new bicycle myself," the boy thinks out loud.

Just then, the boy's mother opens the bedroom door. Belle rushes in, falling over on her back for belly rubs at the little boy's feet.

"Would you please pay attention to this dog," says the mother. "You know I can't stand it when she whines."

Quickly, the boy stuffs Belle's ID tags and reward sign back in the secret box.

"What have you got there," asks his mother.

"Nothing," the boy answers.

The mother leaves. Belle whimpers. The boy looks down at her. Belle gives him her saddest, little lost puppy look. The boy can no longer be angry with her. He reaches over and tickles Belle's belly.

"Okay, Belle," says the boy. "You *are* better to have than a new bicycle."

Chapter Six: Belle Goes Home

More time passes and the curly-haired boy's parents are losing their patience with Belle. Belle still gets up at six o'clock each morning and whines several times during the day. The mother is also losing her patience with the boy because he is forgetting to feed Belle and complains when he must brush her or let her out.

"I don't think I can take this much longer," the mother tells the boy. "At first I thought Belle just missed her people and that she'd stop crying when she got used to us. I know she likes us, but I think we should give her to somebody she can be happy with all of the time."

The boy is very sad to hear this. He knows his mother is serious. He knows where Belle belongs. She isn't really his. He dognapped her. He knows what he must do. He goes to his bedroom and gets Belle's ID tags from the secret box where he hid them. He remembers the reward and takes the folded sign out too.

"If I bring this with me when I bring Belle back, I can get the money and buy a bicycle," says the boy to himself. "But a bicycle doesn't make up for losing Belle. Mom and Dad probably won't let me take the money when they find out I took Belle." He takes the ID tags and reward sign to his mother.

"This is where Belle belongs," the boy says as he hands them to his mother.

"You mean to tell me you had this all along, young man?" his mother asks.

"I'm sorry. I just wanted Belle so much."

"Put these tags on her collar. We're taking her home right now."

Meanwhile, back at Belle's house, Mommy, Grandma, Grandpa, and Nanny are all beginning another lonely day. Today is the loneliest day of all since Belle has been lost. Today is Belle's fourth birthday.

"If only I had gotten up a little earlier to play with Belle before work," Mommy says, as she and her family eat breakfast.

"I could have given up one game show or one soap opera to spend some time with her," Grandma confesses.

Grandpa stops reading the Sunday paper to say, "I shouldn't have played so rough with her. She's just a little dog."

"It's my fault too," admits Nanny, waiting to clean the breakfast dishes as soon as the family is done eating. "I should have taken time to throw a ball for Belle or toss a stick. I could have finished my cleaning afterward. And I shouldn't have called her those mean names."

"If she was here," says Nanny, "she would be my little Belly Button, my sweet little Belly Donut."

Everyone agrees they would act differently if they had a second chance. They had been blessed with the most friendly, adorable, playful dog, and yet, they'd been so busy that Belle was sad and lonely enough to run away.

You see, they thought that Belle had run away because she felt unloved. They didn't know she'd been dognapped. They didn't know they had put ads in the lost pet page of a newspaper the boy with the curly hair and his parents didn't read. They didn't know the boy had taken down all the reward signs they'd put up. How could they?

As they finish breakfast, the doorbell rings. Mommy gets up to answer it.

"I don't believe it," she shouts when she open the door. "It's Belle! Come quickly, everybody! It's Belle!"

Belle runs into the arms of Mommy. Everyone gathers around. Then, crying with joy, they each hug and kiss Belle again and again while she licks them all.

"Please, do come in," says Mommy to the little boy and his parents after they all calm down a bit.

"We've been taking care of her for the past

few months," the boy's mother explains. "If I had known she belonged to you, we would have returned her a long time ago. I just found out today that my son had hidden Belle's ID tags from me."

All the grownups look down at the boy. He mumbles, "I know I was wrong, but I wanted Belle so much. She is the most friendly, adorable, playful dog. She's the best dog ever!"

"We know that now," says Grandpa, as he rubs Belle's belly.

"And we'll never forget it," promises Mommy.

"It's Belle's birthday today," Grandma shares. She looks to the boy and his parents and asks, "Do you want to help us celebrate?"

"Oh, Mommy, can we?" pleads the boy.

"We certainly can," his mother responds.

"Well," says Nanny, "I have to go clean my kitchen floor."

"Nanny," Mommy says, pointing to Belle.

Nanny remembers the promises everyone made over breakfast to treat Belle differently if they had a second chance.

"Right after the party, of course," says Nanny.

Everyone laughs.

During the celebration, they all agree that Belle should live with her mommy, grandparents, and Nanny. They agree they will all keep their promises to pay more attention to Belle. The boy with the curly hair doesn't receive the $500 reward, but it's agreed he can come to play with Belle after school and on weekends. And that's exactly what he does.

Mommy, Grandma, Grandpa, and Nanny are happy Belle is home. Belle is happy too. She is home with her family and has the curly-haired boy for playing. The boy's mother and father are happy Belle no longer wakes them up so early. The boy is happy too. He gets to see Belle often.

Of course, without the reward he did not get

a new bicycle. But I don't think he deserves it. Do
you?

Afterword

Author Christina J. Donato adopted Belle from the North Shore Animal League of America when she was 6 weeks old.

You can find out more about NSAL and their efforts to rescue animals at animalleague.org.

For more adventures about Belle, check the publisher's Facebook page: facebook.com/lhapcjd

Book Two

The Dog Who Wanted to be Human

Dedication

This book is dedicated to my father, Joe Donato, who never stopped encouraging me to write.

Chapter One: Meet Grady

Grady is a black and white bagle, which means he is part beagle and part basset hound. He has big brown eyes and freckles on his nose. He also has big and bouncy, delightfully droopy, super silky ears. Everyone he meets wants to pet him.

He lives with his family: Mommy Christina, Papa Ralph, and twin sisters Mia Daniella and Ava Angelina.

Grady takes a lot of naps. He can curl up and nap in a lot of places. Sometimes he naps on the big couch in the den. Sometimes he naps on the blue dog bed in the den. Sometimes he naps on the small couch in the den. Sometimes he naps on the medium-sized couch in the living room. Sometimes he naps in his crate in the sun room. Sometimes he naps on the red dog bed in the twin's bedroom. Sometimes he naps on the big bed in Mommy Christina's and Papa Ralph's bedroom. Sometimes he naps on Mia Daniella's or Ava Angelina's bed.

Twice a day his family fills his bowls with dog food and water. At least once a day Mommy Christina or one of his sisters take him for a walk. On warm days he spends hours soaking up the sun in his fully fenced backyard.

Grady also enjoys playing ball. His family throws it. He chases it. Grady is supposed to retrieve it, but no matter how much his family begs him, Grady never brings it back. Sometimes his family chases Grady all over the backyard, laughing and laughing until they can't laugh anymore.

"How wonderful you are, Grady," his family tells him. Then, they make a fuss over him and give him a treat.

Grady gets so excited when they play that he howls, "Aroo! Aroo! Aroo!"

Mia Daniella calls this Grady's singing. This makes Ava Angelina laugh. Whenever Grady sings, the twins fuss over him and give him treats.

Grady is so happy when he is eating his treats, that he wags his tail back and forth, hitting anything in its way.

"That Grady can sure keep a steady beat with that tail," Papa Ralph likes to say.

"He sure can," Mommy Christina agrees, as she makes a fuss over Grady and gives him another treat.

Grady often runs around the yard very fast doing "zoomies." Grady loves to run and roll around on the ground. He rolls over the grass, the dirt, the mud, the twigs, the weeds, the plants, and anything else in the yard - even if it is stinky. When that happens, it is bath time. He does not have a choice. He does not like baths (or getting his nails cut, or getting his hair brushed), so he always tries to jump out of the tub. Mommy Christina or Papa Ralph always catch him and back into the bathtub Grady goes.

Afterward, Mommy Christina, Papa Ralph, Mia Daniella, and Ava Angelina give Grady lots of hugs and kisses. They say, "You smell so good, Grady! You are extra soft, and your big and bouncy, delightfully droopy ears are super silky." Grady always gets a treat after a bath – even if he behaves badly.

Grady has a rather good life. All he is expected to do are a few things. He is expected to be cute and cuddly (easy-peasy). He is expected to protect his family. Grady barks whenever a person, a dog, or even a leaf passes by the window. He is expected to do whatever his family tells him. Being smart, he knows the sit, stay, come, down, leave it, off, and heel commands. Whenever he does these things, he gets praises and a treat. When he isn't doing these things, he naps. What else is there to do?

It is all good. Well, almost.

Like a lot of dogs, Grady lives for food. And the food he wants most is what his family eats.

On Sundays, Mommy Christina cooks pasta for dinner, along with meatballs, sausage, and garlic bread dripping with butter. Grady stays right there by Mommy Christina's side as she cooks and serves the meal. He enjoys the aromas and gets very hungry. Grady tilts his head and lifts a front paw, staring at Mommy Christina. To Grady's great disappointment he is always told, "You can't have any, Grady. Garlic is bad for dogs."

Grady loves the summer when his family is outside playing. Papa Ralph barbeques big, juicy burgers on the grill. He serves them with lots of onions. Oh boy! They smell great! It makes Grady hungry. As always, when his family is eating, Grady tilts his head, lifts a front paw, and stares. Sometimes he thinks that perhaps he will have better luck if he lifts his *other* front paw or tilts his head the *other* way. Nope. Papa Ralph always says, "You can't have any, Grady. Onions are bad for dogs."

On Mia Daniella's and Ava Angelina's birthday, the girls always have a big, chocolate cake with lots of thick, pink frosting. Grady watches his family enjoy the birthday cake. His mouth waters. He tilts his head to one side, lifts a front paw, and stares at his sisters. Once again, to Grady's dismay, Mia Daniella tells him, "You can't have any, Grady. Chocolate is bad for dogs."

While it was true that Grady gets his very own big bone to chew on for his "Gotcha Day" (that is the day the family adopted him), he would prefer to have cake.

Chapter Two: Watch Your Food

Grady so very much wishes he could be a boy. He wants to be just like the rest of his family. Then he can eat whatever he wants.

It's not as if Grady has never tried to take food. He ate a batch of Christmas cookies one year. They were shaped like letters, spelling out "Feliz Navidad". Ava Angelina and Mia Daniella baked them because they were learning to speak Spanish. The girls had placed them on the table around the nativity set.

Not long after that, while a Super Bowl party was going on in the den, Grady chowed down on a meatloaf that was placed too close to the edge of the buffet table. To Grady's great shock, into the garbage it went!

Once, Grady happily helped himself to a bowl of strawberry ice cream that Papa Ralph had put down on a step when he went to answer the door. When Grady was caught, Papa Ralph grabbed the ice cream from him and threw it in the garbage bin. Poor Grady was offended to see that happen. Hadn't Papa Ralph put the ice cream down where Grady could reach it?

There was another time when Grady pulled a full loaf of bread, bag and all, off of the kitchen table. He had dragged it into his crate and started tearing it apart before he was caught by his parents, and it was taken away.

Grady was also caught drinking water out of Mommy Christina's glass. He didn't understand why that upset her. They were family and he drinks water all the time.

One time Grady and his beagle friend Chipper tried to steal food that was dangerous for them to eat. The family's backyard had grape vines growing along the fence. Grady was having a playdate with his friend. Mommy Christina saw Chipper pulling down on the grapevines while Grady ate the grapes on them. At first, Mommy Christina thought this was cute and funny. She was going to grab her camera and take a video. Something inside her told her to look up on the computer to see if grapes could make dogs sick. She found out that grapes could kill dogs.

The very next day all the grapevines were removed from the backyard.

It's not even *just* garlic, onions, ice cream, bread, chocolate, and grapes that his family eats but refuses to share with Grady. They also tell him he can't have alcohol; apple seeds; apricot

pits; avocados; bacon; cherry pits; coconut; coffee, tea, and other caffeine; fat trimmings and bones; macadamia nuts; milk and dairy; mushrooms; mustard seeds; peach pits; persimmons; plums; raisins; raw dough, eggs, meat, and fish; rhubarb leaves; rosemary; stems, leaves, peels and seeds of citrus plants; sugary foods and drinks; walnuts; and anything sweetened with xylitol.

Whew! That is quite a list for a dog that is always hungry and wants to eat anything that looks or smells good.

So, day after day, meal after meal, Grady sits by his family: head tilted, front paw up. Not working? Tilt head the other way. Switch paws. And night after night, as Grady falls asleep on any one of three couches, two dog beds, one crate, or three human beds, he wishes he were a boy.

Chapter Three: Changes

One day Grady is awoken by the sound of Mommy Christina's voice.

"Time to get up, everybody! Breakfast is ready! Let's get this day started!"

Grady begins to stand up and stretch.

"Whoa!" Grady exclaims to himself, "Where are my four legs and four paws? Where is my fur? I have legs, arms, feet, and hands. I have skin and hair."

Grady rushes to the closest mirror. *"I'm a boy*!! The hair on my head is still short and black. I still have big, brown eyes. I still have freckles on my nose. And... and... my ears are still big, just not bouncy, delightfully droopy, and super silky anymore. *I am a boy*!!!!"

Grady rushes to the kitchen table.

Mommy Christina is surprised. "Who is this? Could this be our Grady?"

Papa Ralph practically falls off his chair. "I believe it is. Wow! How wonderful this is for us!"

The twins do not know what to make of this development. Is it wonderful? Should they be happy? What does this mean for them?

Grady is excited to be a boy. This very morning, Grady finally gets to eat the family's food.

Right away Ava Angelina asks Papa Ralph if Grady will have to do his share of the chores now that he is a boy.

"Of course," says Papa Ralph.

Mommy Christina agrees. "He will go to school, do his homework and do his chores."

Grady is told he will mow the lawn in the summer and shovel snow in the winter. He will have to pick up after himself, put his toys away, clear his dirty dishes from the table, and keep his bedroom neat and tidy.

Grady asks, "Will I get treats if I do what I am told? I always got treats when I was a good dog."

"I guess so," says Mommy Christina.

Grady is so happy to hear that. He does what he is told, every single time. He *loves* treats, especially ones for humans.

At mealtime, Grady's appetite is so big that he usually has two or three helpings of food. He even eats more than Papa Ralph!

Grady learns what he thought is true – foods that look good and smell good also taste good and can be good for growing boys.

The very next day after becoming a human boy, Grady goes to school. His teacher introduces him to the other students. As Grady goes to find a seat, he hears snickering.

A voice from the back of the class shouts, "Sit back here. With those big and bulky, dorky, droopy, super silly ears you won't have any problem hearing."

There is more snickering. The teacher tells everyone to hush. Grady finds a seat somewhere in the middle.

At mid-day, the teacher announces it is time to go to the cafeteria for lunch. Grady eagerly follows his classmates there. You see, even though Grady ate the lunch Mommy Christina packed for him while he was on the bus on the way to school, he is hungry again.

Grady follows Mia Daniella and Ava Angelina to the sisters' usual table. He tilts his head to one side and lifts an arm like he did when he had four legs and paws.

"What are you doing," Ava Angelina asks.

"I'm begging you to let me have some of your lunch," says Grady.

"Stop doing that with your head and arm. You are embarrassing us," says Mia Daniella.

"If you don't share your lunch," says Grady, "I will go around to every table and beg for food."

Mia Daniella whispers to Ava Angelina, "I think he means it. If he does that, everyone will laugh at us for having such a weird brother."

"I heard that," Grady exclaims, tilting his head the other way, and lifting his other arm.

"Of course you did," says Mia Daniella. "How can you not hear everything with those big and bulky, dorky, droopy, super silly ears of yours?"

Mia Daniella and Ava Angelina each give Grady half of their lunches.

From now on, Mommy Christina packs two lunches for Grady. One she gives to Grady to eat on the bus on the way to school and the other lunch she gives to one of the twins for Grady to eat at lunchtime.

That Sunday, Mommy Christina cooks the family's big Sunday lunch of pasta with meatballs and sausage, with a side of garlic bread dripping with butter. By now Mommy Christina is getting wise to Grady. She makes two loaves of garlic bread dripping with butter. One is just for Grady. The other is for the rest of the family to share.

The next weekend the weather is warm and sunny. Papa Ralph decides to barbecue burgers on the grill for everyone.

"Two for me, please," Grady shouts happily, "with lots of onions!"

"You've got it, Grady," replies Papa Ralph.

Grady enjoys every bite.

A couple of weeks later Ava Angelina says to Mommy Christina, "Tomorrow is Grady's 'Gotcha Day'. Should we make it his birthday and have a party?"

Grady overhears this and comes running.

"Grady," says Mommy Christina, "since it is your birthday, what kind of cake do you want?"

Grady doesn't even have to think for a second. He knows just what he wants: a big chocolate cake with lots of thick, fudgy, frosting.

That is what he gets. And he enjoys every bite.

During his party, Grady notices that Mommy Christina and Papa Ralph are enjoying cups of coffee with their cake. It smells good. Grady asks for a cup.

"Sorry, Grady," responds Mommy Christina. "Coffee isn't good for children."

It surprises Grady to hear this. He thought that all human food is good for all humans. He is disappointed to learn this is not true.

Seeing Grady's disappointment, Mommy Christina explains, "There are many human foods that are not good for children, such as alcohol, and caffeinated drinks like coffee and tea. Some things may look good to eat but are poisonous to all humans such as toadstools and holly berries. People can also have food allergies that can cause them great harm.

"Wow," says Grady. "I thought humans can eat anything they want, whenever they want, as much as they want."

Chapter Four: Always in Trouble

It isn't just learning how not all human foods are good to eat that makes being a boy not as great as Grady had expected.

One day at school, a boy who is much bigger than Grady grabs Grady's apple. Grady bites him! He just bites the boy's hand without giving it a second thought. Grady is sent to the school's principal. The principal makes Grady sit still and think about what he did.

Grady still loves to chase balls when his class is playing baseball. Just as when he was a dog, Grady never thinks to return the ball. He holds on to it. This does not work out well in baseball, as Grady soon learns.

His teammates shout to Grady, "Throw the ball to first!" Then they shout, "Throw the ball to second." Then they shout, "Throw the ball to third!" Lastly, they shout, "Throw the ball home!"

Of course, Grady doesn't. So, whenever Grady catches the ball in a baseball game, the batter and any runners on the bases score home runs. This makes the children on his team terribly angry. As much as he tries, Grady just can't understand. He always did this as a dog and would be fussed over and receive a treat. Now when he runs around the outfield he is chased by his own teammates. Grady falls on the ground and rolls around on the grass, dirt, and mud, holding on to the baseball with all his might.

Every time Grady does this, Mommy Christina makes Grady scrub himself clean in the bathtub and wash his hair. Mommy Christina even makes Grady wash his uniform and go to bed straight after supper without dessert. You can imagine how upset Grady feels to not have dessert. Mommy Christina tells Grady that while it is expected he will get dirty playing sports; he is not allowed to get extra dirty on purpose. He needs to clean up his messes on his own.

It isn't just in baseball where Grady's dog behaviors don't work out now that he is a boy.

Since as a dog Grady enjoyed aroo'ing, it makes sense that he might enjoy singing as a boy. The problem is Grady sings too loudly and out of tune. This means that whenever Grady sings, others hold their ears, tell him he is awful, and tell him to keep quiet. That is not fun for Grady.

Because Grady had been so good at keeping a beat with his tail (when he had one), he thinks he might like to play the drums in the school band. When he auditions, the music teacher is impressed with Grady's steady beat and lets him join. However, when it comes to rehearsals with the rest of the children, Grady bangs on the drums as hard as he can, drowning out all the other musicians. This is just not acceptable behavior. Once again, conduct that was rewarded when he was a dog gets him in trouble as a boy.

There is one more thing that gets Grady in trouble again and again – napping. Whenever Grady is made to sit still and be quiet, he quickly falls asleep. Grady had always been a napper, and he still is.

It doesn't matter if he is in class, or watching a movie with his family, or in the audience at Mia Daniella's school play, or listening to Ava Angelina performing in the school orchestra, or during story time at the local public library. If Grady is sitting still, he is napping.

To make matters worse, Grady snores. His family thought it was cute when he was a dog. They do not think so now that Grady is a boy. He is told time and time again that napping and snoring in public are rude and distracting.

When Grady naps at school, his teachers send him to see the principal. After being sent to see the principal a few times, the principal calls Mommy Christina and Papa Ralph, asking them to come to the school for a chat.

The principal tells Grady's parents that it isn't just the napping. Everything Grady does he does too loudly. He shouts too loudly. He sings too loudly. He bangs on the drums too loudly. And for sure he snores too loudly. It seems that Grady wants to do what he wants, when he wants, for as long as he wants.

Papa Ralph and Mommy Christina had suspected this is what the principal wanted to talk about. Grady is the same way at home. They have come prepared. Mommy Christina hands the principal a family photo of when Grady was still a dog.

"You may not believe what I am going to tell you," Papa Ralph begins, "but Grady used to be our family dog."

Looking at the photograph the principal says, "I can see the resemblance – short black hair, big brown eyes, freckles on his nose, and those ears! But Grady is a boy now and he must act like a boy."

Mommy Christina and Papa Ralph tell the principal they are doing the best they can. Grady is just being himself, except that his "self" has changed.

Since becoming a boy, Grady does not like being the center of attention. As a dog, getting attention meant getting fussed over and getting treats. As a boy, getting attention means getting in trouble. And what's more, Grady no longer has much time to play or nap. Grady is expected to only sleep on his own bed. He gets in trouble and is punished if he screams at anything or anyone who passes by the house.

Grady is just protecting his family. No one seemed to mind before when he was a dog.

Chapter Five: Be Careful What You Wish

Things change the most for Grady with his sisters Mia Daniella and Ava Angelina. Instead of playing with Grady and fussing over him, they fight with him and make fun of his ears. His ears! Grady can't help that he has big ears. No one seemed to mind when he was a dog.

To Grady, it doesn't seem as if things can get any worse until they do. One day Papa Ralph brings home a squiggly, wiggly, cutely cuddly, fun, and furry puppy. The family has so very much missed having a dog.

Another dog! How can they?

That new puppy has a good life. He can curl up and nap on any one of three couches, two dog beds, one crate, or four human beds. That includes Grady's bed. Twice a day his family fills the puppy's bowls with dog food and water. At least once a day Mommy Christina or one of the twins takes the puppy for a walk. On warm days, the puppy spends hours soaking up the sun in the fenced backyard.

That puppy has some nerve. All the puppy is expected to do is to be cute and cuddly, protect his family, and obey commands. That puppy thinks he is so smart because he knows the commands sit, stay, come, down, leave it, off, and heel. Whenever he does these things, the puppy gets a treat. Mia Daniella and Ava Angelina stroke the puppy's big and bouncy, delightfully droopy, super silky ears and say how wonderful they are.

Grady learns that going to school, doing homework, and doing chores is a lot harder than looking cute and cuddly, barking to protect his family, and obeying a few commands.

The only good thing – the only high point – is that Grady gets to eat tasty food. In fact, in between meals, when no one else is around, Grady helps himself to all the snacks his hands can hold.

And he eats. And he eats. And he eats. He just cannot stop himself. It is all so good.

As time passes, Grady eats so much food that his stomach grows bigger and bigger. And he gets tummy aches.

His tummy gets so big and hurts so much that Grady *explodes*! The moment he explodes he is startled awake only to find out that he has been dreaming.

"I have four legs and four paws again!" Grady thinks to himself with glee. "I have fur!"

Grady rushes to the closest mirror.

"I still have short black hair, big brown eyes, and freckles on my nose. And... and... my ears are still big and bouncy, delightfully droopy, and super silky. *I'm still a dog! I am still me!!!*"

From that day forward Grady happily does the things he does best. He is cute and cuddly (easy-peasy). He protects his family. Grady barks whenever a person, dog, or even a leaf passes by the window. He does whatever he is told. Being smart, he knows the commands sit, stay, come, down, leave it, off, and heal.

Whenever he does these things, he gets praises and treats. When he isn't doing these things, he naps. What else was there to do?

And Grady is a very, very, very, happy dog.

Afterword

Author Christina J. Donato adopted Grady when he was two and a half years old from B.O.N.E.S., the Beagles of New England States.

You can find out more about B.O.N.E.S. and their efforts to rescue beagles at bonesbeagles.org.

For more adventures about Grady, check the publisher's Facebook page: "Left-handed Author Publishing."

Acknowledgements

It has been a long journey to publishing this book.

My parents, Joe and Jane Donato always supported my love of writing and my desire to be an author. My path may have detoured greatly, but they always had faith in me and my God-given love for the written word.

Many thanks go out to my long-time love, Ralph Walton, and my friends and family who have encouraged me along the way.

I must express my gratitude to my editor, Ellie Davis of Pressque Publishing, LLC. It can be difficult to judge your own writing. I know Ellie's input has made my books better.

I especially thank my illustrator, Alex, for bringing my characters and their stories, real and imagined, from inside my head to the page in glorious color.

Psalm 36:6c Contemporary English Version
"...all people and animals are under Your [God's] care"

Photos of the Real Belle

8 weeks old

Christmas, 2 years

Playing with balloon, 11 months old

11 years old

Photos of the Real Grady

Ralph, Grady, & Mommy Christina – 2012
Struminsky Professional Photography, RI & New England

Grady sharing one of the "3 couches" with his *B.O.N.E.S. foster brother,* Tracker – 2013

Happy 5th birthday – 2014

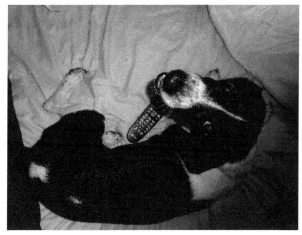

Grady taking over one of the "3 human beds" – 2015

Excuse me – I'm napping here! – 2016

Begging – 2017

Hoping for some food at a
Café – 2018

Enjoying a treat and a massage
at the 2019 Annual B.O.N.E.S.
Beagle Bash

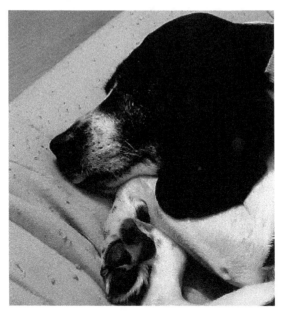

Napping with his tongue out – 2020

Photobombing while begging
(again!) for some of Mommy
Christina's food - 2021

CPSIA information can be obtained
at www.ICGtesting.com
Printed in the USA
BVHW051228251021
619811BV00018BA/566